MAMA,
COMING
AND
GOING

JUDITH CASELEY

Mama, Coming and Going

Greenwillow Books, New York

Watercolor paints and colored pencils
were used for the full-color art.
The text type is Quadrata.

Printed in Singapore by Tien Wah Press
First Edition
1 2 3 4 5 6 7 8 9 10

Library of Congress Cataloging-in Publication Data

Caseley, Judith.
Mama, coming and going / by Judith Caseley.
p. cm.
Summary: Big sister Jenna recalls the funny things
that Mama forgot to do after baby Mickey was born.
ISBN 0-688-11441-5 (trade).
ISBN 0-688-11442-3 (lib. bdg.)
[1. Babies—Fiction.   2. Mother and child—Fiction.
3. Memory—Fiction.]   I. Title.
PZ7.C2677Mam 1994
[E]—dc20
92-29402 CIP AC

To Queen Jenna,

with all my love

After Jenna's baby brother was born,
Mama did some funny things.
She remembered to read Jenna her
books at bedtime. But she forgot
to defrost the chicken for dinner.

So they had pizza instead.

She remembered Mickey's bathtime.
But when the doorbell rang, and Jenna cut her
finger, and Mickey spit up all over the couch,
Mama forgot she left the water running.

So Jenna went wading in her rainboots.
"Don't waste water," she told Mama.

Mama laughed and said she felt just like a
chicken running around without a head.
"What do you mean?" said Jenna.
"I mean," said Mama, "that I don't know
whether I'm coming or going."

So Jenna drew a picture of Mama running around without a head, and made Mama laugh again.

Mama wrote a thank-you note to Aunt Mary for
the nifty overalls she'd sent Mickey.
Aunt Mary called Mama on the telephone and
said, "I never sent him any such thing." And she
asked Mama how come she named a boy
Mickey, since it reminded her of a mouse.

So Jenna drew Mickey a picture of a mouse
because Aunt Mary had forgotten him.

Once when Mama was in a rush, she shut
the car door and locked Mickey inside, along
with the car keys on the front seat.
While Mama had her fist in her mouth, Jenna
saw Mr. Carbone and yelled, "Help!"
He took one look at Mickey, winked, and
went away. He came back with a hanger.

Jenna danced for Mickey and made him smile
while Mr. Carbone unlocked the door.
Mama scooped up Mickey and gave him a hug.
Then she kissed Jenna and said, "You're such a
big help, honey."
"It was fun," said Jenna.

Another time Mama
and Jenna and Mickey
drove to the drugstore
for diapers and to
the supermarket
for baby food.
Mama put all of the
packages in the back
of the station wagon.

Then they walked to
the library, where Mickey
chewed on the books,
so they had to leave.

When they got back to the car, Mama had left it
wide open. She said burglars must have been
too scared to steal anything, because only a nut
would leave her car open.

Jenna said maybe they didn't like to wear diapers
or eat baby food. She and Mama laughed
so loudly that it made Mickey cry.

One hot summer day Mama dragged Jenna from
the pool and dressed her in party clothes and stuck
Mickey in his car seat and put her sun hat on top
of the car while she combed out Jenna's hair.

Then they drove to Albert's birthday party at the
Party Palace. Mickey got cranky, so Mama handed
Jenna toys and Jenna tossed them back to Mickey
and Mickey threw them back at Jenna, which kept
him happy.
"Look for a street sign that starts with an M," Mama
said to Jenna, who was just starting to read.

They drove and drove until they heard a bang.
Jenna said, "The car is smoking," and Mama
said, "What next?" as she pulled the car over
to the curb.
Mickey started to scream, and they got out
of the car.

"Look, Mama," said Jenna, and there was the
sign that said Middleneck Road.
Mama put Mickey in the carriage and
remembered the present, and Mickey
stopped screaming and patted the bushes
all the way down the street.

They reached the Party Palace and went inside.
"Hello," said Mama. "We're here for Albert's party."
"No carriages allowed," said a lady, so Mama
took the carriage outside and unstrapped Mickey.
Then she went back inside and put him on the
floor. Jenna kept him from pulling ceramic statues
off the shelves.

"We're here for Albert's party," Mama said again.
The lady said, "What's the last name?"
Jenna told her "Lee," while Mama looked for
the invitation.
"That's next week," said the lady, and Mama just
stood there.

Then she grabbed up Mickey, and she took
Jenna's hand, and they walked outside. The sun
was hotter than before, and Mama said, "Where
did I leave my sun hat?" She looked as if she
was about to cry.

"I think you left it on top of the car," said Jenna.

They passed a shop that smelled nice when
the door opened, and Mama took them inside.

Mama made a telephone call, and they sat
down at a pretty table with flowers on it.
"May I help you?" said a smiling lady.

Mama whispered in her ear. The lady disappeared
and came back with two cupcakes. There was
a candle on Jenna's, and the lady lit it. They sang
"Happy Birthday" to Albert, even though Mama
said they would go to his party next week.
Then they ate the cupcakes.

"Who called for a tow truck?" said a man
from the doorway, and Mama said, "I did!"
He hooked up their car, and Jenna and
Mickey and Mama had their first tow
truck ride ever.

They even took a taxi home from the
auto repair shop.
While Mama paid the driver, Jenna
and Mickey played on the grass.

And that's where Jenna found Mama's sun hat.

"I don't know if I'm coming or going," said
Mama when she saw it. Then she took the
hat and placed it on Jenna's head.
"Queen Jenna," she said. "What would I do
without you?"
Jenna smiled. Then she took the hat off
and put it on Mama.
"Queen Mama," she said. "Coming or going."